Desert Dusk Music

DESERT DUSK *music*

—— A LOVE STORY ——

THOMAS TIMMINS

ZOËTOWN MEDIA
HAYDENVILLE, MA

ISBN 978-0-9970287-2-0
Printed in the United States of America

Published by Zoëtown® Media
Zoëtown is a registered trademark of Zoëtown Media.
Haydenville, MA
www.thomastimmins.com

Cover art by James Johnson-Corwin
Line drawings of desert fauna by Roger Hall Scientific Illustration,
Oakland, CA 94605 www.inkart.net
Book and cover design by Maureen Moore, Booksmyth Press
www.thebooksmythpress.com

For Janina, a true friend

Contents

Desert Dusk Music

The fox

She'd been ill, "way sick," she wrote, lying in a sweat on her maroon couch in her single-wide trailer in the desert foothills. She couldn't remember when she'd felt so bad. Across her fragile garden, her husband hauled stone for their new house. Building their house from scratch, he wished he'd had an easier recipe. "At least I've got you home during the week," he said, setting out the cat food for the fox they're taming. Her email ended, "Ron took the fox into the vet this morning. Poor thing. She's hot, barely breathing. Like me."

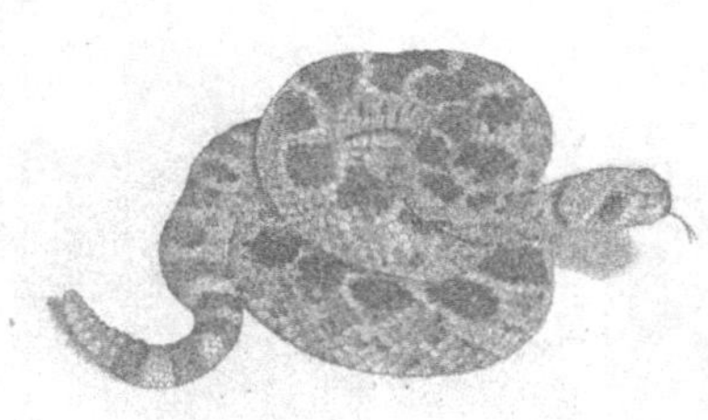

Leaving for church

Before she and Karl left to tour the magical church in the mountains, she tried on her new white silk dress in front of the dim bathroom mirror. "Who is this?" Twirling, she said aloud to her trimmed, hennaed coif, "Adios, Miss Natural." The door chimes rang like merry-go-round pipes. All she had for shoes were her old, scuffed Tevas, her companions in years of travel from Atlanta to Daramsala and back. Her monk shoes. No match for the dress. "Where's Ron?" Karl asked. "Building Supply. Needs hinges." He said, "Ready?" She kicked off her sandals and took his arm.

The job

Later I found out I was no different than everyone I worked with–trapped inside the windowless building, we all hated our jobs. We all had our own ways of coping. Shana took her computer home, wired into office email, pretending she worked for herself. Cyndi wore pink, letting her California nipples show through. Her boss stuttered when he talked to her. I groaned to the mountains every morning. "Life's a gift. Life's a gift." I'd shudder and climb the stairs to practice deep breathing. "How do you do this, day after day?" I asked my friend. She shrugged. "Money."

Feeling good

"When you've been sick a while, you don't remember what feeling good is like." We were walking toward the city park, the only public place where we could sit on green grass. "You mean sick in your body? Or sick in your head?" I wondered if there was any difference. I could run a 10K, didn't smoke or drink, but so what? "I mean the body." She took my hand, lacing our fingers. "Is this feeling good?" I asked, squeezing. "It's a beginning." I said "It feels good in my head." She squinted up at me and tousled my hair.

Miracle dirt

I in my shorts, she in her silky white dress, we knelt down in the church sanctuary, our bare knees scraping on gravelly 'miracle dirt'. I scraped up some amber powder and rained it onto her open palm. "Where will you sprinkle it?" "I need it for the new house. Maybe over the door, so it drops on my head. I'm not sure I can move in." "What? You've sacrificed everything for that house. Years of scrounging money, living in a trailer ...." She said, "My sacrifice ... almost killed me. I need a resurrection." Her thigh moved against mine.

Best friend

I spend too much time on the phone. Not that I don't love talking to people, I do. I really do. As long as we can hang up. Hanging out's different. Another experience I reserve for a few. Well, maybe not a few. I have a big family and they're mostly fun to be with. Ron has two friends he spends time with, besides me. I'm his 'best friend.' I like that, but he's not my 'best friend.' He's my friend, my lifetime companion, but not even Jeannie is my best friend. I'm not sure I have a best friend.

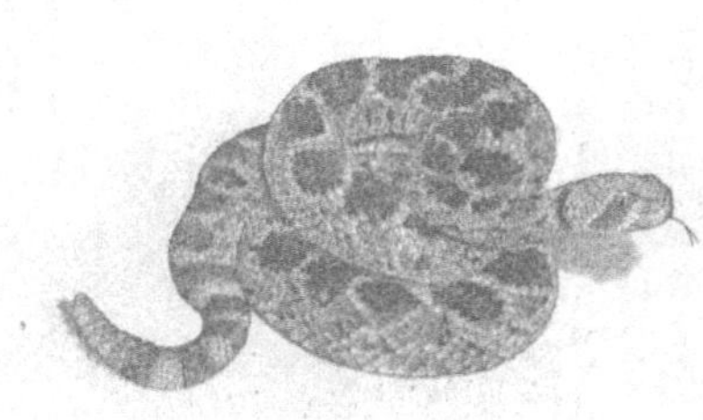

Eyes

Karl paints eyes. People's eyes, cat's eyes, dog's eyes. Any animal or fish. He paints eyes that don't see like eyes on butterfly wings or eyes in the center of boles. He wants to paint my eyes. A way of luring me into his studio. I'm not ready. "Take my photo," I said. "I need to see the moisture that could change to tears any second. I need to see the glow of my tiger orchids in your whites. I need to look into your soul when I paint." I smiled, putting my shades on over my soul's eyes.

Paint

Once you'd seen those sienna pools set into the narrow crevasse between her high tanned cheekbones and sharp eyebrows sheltering a mischievous soul who promised she'd be up for anything ... even you, friend - may I call you friend? - especially you, like me, would feel your imagination erupt from your heart in images of dropping anchor in dusky warm coves and come what may, baring your every hunger and desire, risking everything for her. All I wanted was to paint her eyes. If she'd calmed down and stared out the window behind me and let me paint ....

Intense beginning

All I wanted was to pretend I was 11 again, a happy girl, dressed in Easter white, showing off to my girlfriends at church. He said he'd play along. "My god, you're gorgeous," he said through the car window. If I was so gorgeous, you'd think as soon as he saw me step outside, he'd jump out and run to me. At least he'd open the car door. Then he kissed me on the ear and put his hand on my bare leg. His fingers raised a million goosebumps. I shivered, pulled my dress over my knee, faced away. Hopeless.

Keeping it to yourself

It's better to keep quiet about a big change you're planning. Oh, you can mention something to your best friend, but refuse to discuss it. You should give her a subtle heads-up, so she's not too surprised when your life turns upside down. Don't tell your therapist, don't tell your mother, and, obviously, don't tell your boyfriend or husband. Let the energy build inside you. Keep the lid on. Smile a lot and look at the sky with awe. But keep quiet. Then, you'll feel no outside pressure to make excuses or give reasons. That way, your energy takes over.

The Virgin of Another Chance

When he sent me the photo of me standing outside the church in my white dress, my face freaked me out even more than his caption: The Virgin of Another Chance. Those white teeth. No wrinkles. Gray's coming in and I look like a virgin. You take the virgin and give me my black hair. I want to be a holy woman, but not for Karl. For Ron? I've always been the loyal type. But he doesn't have what I need and my clock runs on high. Karl has two kids. They look like him. His sperm is viable.

A nap

She'll call Monday, after seeing her therapist. At least it's after. If it was before, I'd worry she'd talk about me. Maybe she'll talk about me anyway. I don't care who she talks to or what she says, as long as she keeps coming over. She works too hard – you can see it in the rings under her eyes. She doesn't laugh as much, or maybe I'm not funny anymore. She needs more sleep. I always feel happy after a good sleep. I'll ask if she wants to take a nap with me. Clothes on. We'd both feel better, after.

Names and notes

I call her Belinda. It's not her real name. Or maybe it is, but she said we're a make-believe pair and we get to concoct everything about ourselves. I treasure her child-like attitude. It's a kick since I don't want her to know my real name either, in case she writes something down - and she will. I've seen her sneaking notes into a book she keeps in her pocket. I asked "What did you write? Something about us?" She said, "You'll never know," and winked at me. I grabbed, she caught my hand, and pulled it to her breast.

When she didn't write

When she didn't write back, my mind sailed off into the ghost world where she dropped me because … why? What scared her? Did her husband find out we were … friends? Never more than hugs. If his insecurities triggered hers, or if her hated boss insisted she never be in touch with me, the troublemaker, or she'd lose her job, or if she didn't really care … well, damn, I should have taken her into my bed when I had the chance that night. At least then I'd have a naked image of her carved into my unerodable memories.

Sensitive hands

He has the most beautiful hands. Long fingers, arced tips, black hair shiny as crow's feathers on his knuckles, palms webbed with fine lines. Grinning, he says the tangle of lines means he's ultra-sensitive. He's sensitive, but not the way you'd expect. I say "You're shallow." He shrugs. I tease him until he's turned on, then make a married woman's excuse and split. He smiles. Always eager to see me, never mentions I'm married. Sensitive like the fox. Hangs around after dark, knows when he's getting too close and when it's time to leave. I leave. I keep coming back.

Bow hunters

Ron's out of town for the weekend, bow-hunting with Jordan. Ron doesn't own a bow, but he loves stealthing through the woods, as deer as any buck Jordan's ever downed. Not that it matters where he is. I keep my own comings and goings, he keeps his. But we know where each other is when we're around town. Better he's in those canyons, out of cell range since I won't be home if things work out the way it looks like. I told the painter I'd model tomorrow afternoon. Sometimes he feels creepy, but I'm curious. It's now or never.

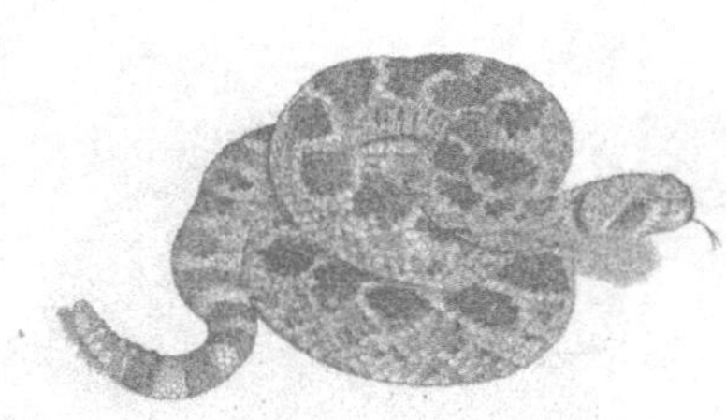

Bicycle exploits

Ron's bicycle trip around the world turned him into an irresistible animal. The first day, I was just out of the river, dripping wet, when his sleek, sculpted body took my breath. I took him to my bed before supper. We chased each other, leaning, drafting, pumping with all we had. We spun out on a curve and crashed, smashing the lamp, spilling melted wax on our shoulders. That was ten years ago and it's been uphill ever since. Now when he brings up his biking exploits, I cringe. He crushed his sperm-maker on his bicycle seat somewhere in China.

Her voice

Her voice resonates in my whole body, calming me, tickling my spirit. My name in her mouth is a stream bubbling over moss. When she lisps, something happy catches in my throat. I swear I'll kiss her tonight and swallow the words in her spit. She'll whisper adagios into my ear, both ears. I call her at work where I hear moist melodies hidden inside her dry voicemail. I've recorded her every voice message to me, all three. She's too discreet, too stingy with words. That will change. She'll talk, growl, moan, scream. It's her whimper will do me in.

Dreaming of peace and light

She's cold. She knows I want her. We'd wake up for leisurely Sunday breakfast, read the papers, dawdle with each other. Laughing about everything, why would we need words? My dream. Or is it my dream? My true dream is noisy, wet, brighter than a halogen spotlight. She's damp, prefers the shade. It's better that way. No one will suspect me of anything. With her I am wide open, upbeat as a fruit seller, optimistic as Jim Lansdale, the preacher who guarantees his whole flock will rise together. In myself, my secret wishes hide, my plan, my deeds, deep down.

Natural hearts

I'll never leave Ron. I need his protection and his natural heart. He adores me even if his soul has never touched my soul. He would if he could. He's smart like a fox, for sure, but the russet beauties we're taming are smart about one thing only, getting their food and getting away. Ron's given me the life of a princess, when I want the world of a queen mother. I'm edging closer to Karl, the dark buck roaming through, maybe leaving me young, then passing on. Ron and I will stay, raising chickens and, someday, maybe, a baby.

I don't get it

I don't get it. She's so edgy lately. Anything I say or do sets her off. This morning all I wanted was to kiss her nipple like I do sometimes when she gets out of the shower, still dripping. First one, then the other, then her chin and eyes. Sometimes we keep going, usually not. Today, she froze like it hurt but she had to put up with it. Her taste gets me through until I see her. I always want to see her. After working all day alone, I want to see her. Lately, she's never home before dark.

The fox can't resist

The fox can't resist the scent of chicken shit. My ladies and their one banty rooster, nine leghorn layers, 3 banties. Little guy's a sperm machine. He crows and leaps on the gals for a quick flutter and squawk. Only one chicken has ever resisted him, an old cluck who went swimming in my stew pot not long after. I told Karl we'd tamed the fox, maybe so much he depended on us for food. I'm thinking of not feeding him. Karl said, "Too late. He's tame enough to hang around until one morning when you count hens, one's missing."

Sunglasses

Karl left his sunglasses in my car. When Ron drove it to town and back he didn't see them. Or say anything to me. He notices everything, so he purposely ignored the matter of the sunglasses. That's okay ... I'm not ready to say anything. Certainly not ready to do anything. I'm getting close. Should I tell Karl what I want from him? He may give it to me with more feeling if he knows. I could cast a spell on him, a love spell laced with freedom and irresponsibility. Men. I won't tell him anything. If it happens ... dreamy ....

Rafting

I've lived here only a few years and the river looks the same to me but they say we're losing it to the millions of throats who believe Phoenix and LA are the solution to their age and their poverty. She loves the river and hates the cities. She mentioned rafting, easy floating to the confluence by nightfall. All I've wanted for months was to make the confluence with her, even just once. She has her own paddle and life jacket. I'll rent the raft and my gear. She promised to bring sandwiches and watermelon if I bring the beer.

Dusk music

I climbed the south rim to watch the sunset. In the silence of a red tail hawk circling, the dense orange sky of sunset began to hum, a high pitch emanating from the horizon, then creeping toward me, leading night's shadow to my feet ... she's on her way. As she nears, the light diminishes and my ears pick up notes spilling across the sand. The flute player has slipped into the valley under the cover of shadows rising. "He's my cousin," she'd said. "When you hear him, it's safe to go out." Something's moving in the dark behind me.